PENNY TO THE RESCUE!

By Casey Neumann

Based on the teleplay "Penny Rescues a Treasure" by Scott Albert

Illustrated by Dave Aikins

A Random House PICTUREBACK® Book

Random House 🏠 New York

rhcbooks.com

ISBN 978-1-9848-4782-9

MANUFACTURED IN CHINA

10 9 8 7 6 5 4 3 2 1

Lenticular cover effect and production: Red Bird Publishing Ltd., U.K.

One day near Shipwreck Cove, Salty was loading his barge with kelp. Penny sat in her Aqua Wing, ready to tow him to the Lemon Shack.

Suddenly, Salty spotted something in the pile of kelp. "It's shiny and yellow—maybe it's treasure!"

In the water nearby, Cap'n Dilly and Matilda overheard Salty.

"Treasure?" Matilda exclaimed.

"*Arrr!* There's nothing pirates like more than treasure!" said Cap'n Dilly.

The two swam closer to get a better view.

Salty picked up the bright yellow object. "Oh, it's just a little lemon. I thought maybe I'd found the treasure of Shipwreck Cove!" He told Penny the story of Captain Greenbeard, who had hidden a treasure so deep in the ocean, no one had found it.

"Maybe I can find it with my Aqua Wing," Penny said excitedly. "I'll take this kelp to the Lemon Shack and then go treasure hunting!"

While Penny was away, the pirate crocodiles used their ship's periscope to hunt for the treasure.

"Do ye see it?" Cap'n Dilly asked Matilda.

She saw something—but it was just a gold-colored fish. "I have a pirate-y plan!" she said. "Let's have Penny find the treasure in her Aqua Wing, and then we'll pirate it from her!"

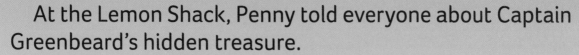

At the Lemon Shack, Penny told everyone about Captain Greenbeard's hidden treasure.

"It's the most valuable treasure a pirate ever *gobba-gobba* tucked away!" gobbled Commodore Smurkturkski. He put Penny in charge of finding it.

She leapt into her Aqua Wing and took off!

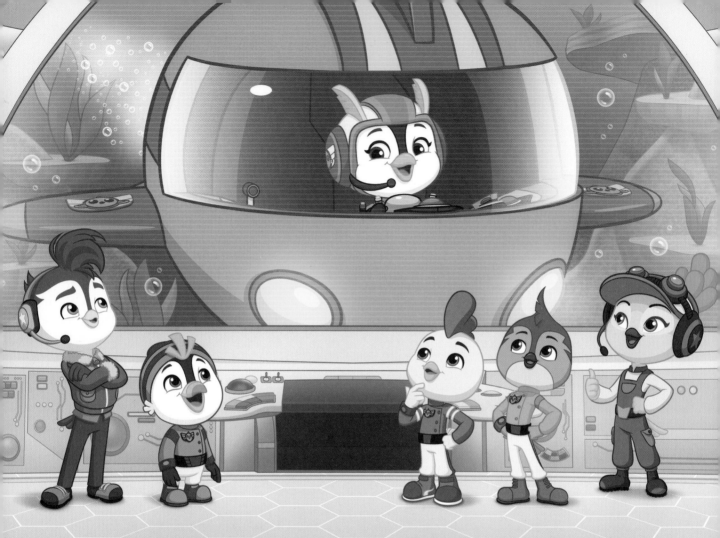

When Penny reached Shipwreck Cove, she got a radio call from Speedy.

"I hear you're in charge of a treasure hunt," he said.

"Yeah!" Penny replied. "Salty said the treasure is really, really deep in the ocean. I hope I can find it."

Bea told Penny the Aqua Wing's metal detector would let her know when she was close to the treasure.

Deep in Shipwreck Cove, the pirate crocodiles trailed behind Penny on her treasure hunt.

"Right on course, Cap'n!" said Matilda.

"And Penny'll get the treasure for us!" Cap'n Dilly chuckled.

Penny activated the Aqua Wing's metal detector, which beeped as she dove deep toward the bottom of the sea.
     "When the beeping gets faster, it means you're very close!" Bea said to Penny through her headset.

Suddenly, the metal detector began to beep faster! Penny steered the Aqua Wing toward a narrow cave in the coral. She gasped. "I think I found something—in that cave!"

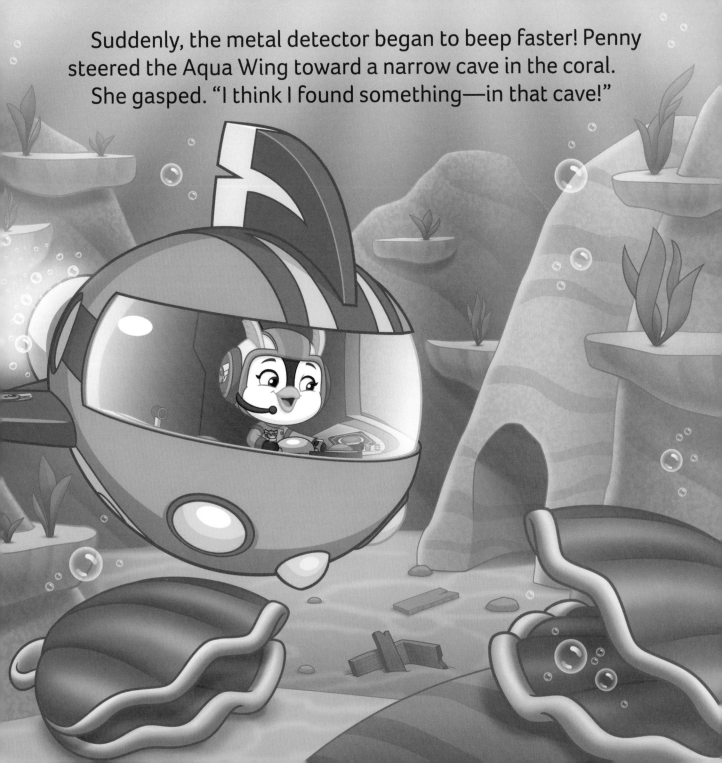

"Penny! Your sub is too big to fit!" radioed Speedy. "Don't worry! I'll use my mini sub!" Penny hopped on and glided into the narrow cave.

"There it is!" she shouted. She used the claws on her mini sub to grab the chest, then darted back out.

Secretly watching Penny from their ship, the two pirates cheered. "She found the treasure!" Matilda shouted.

"*We're so tricky! We're so clever! We'll make the treasure ours forever! Yo-ho-ho! Arrr!*" the pirate crocs sang.

"It be time for the rest of the plan," said Cap'n Dilly. "Pretend ye need rescuing, Matilda."

On the ocean's surface, Commodore Smurkturkski was paddling his rowboat to check on Penny when he saw a crocodile struggling in the water! He immediately called the Top Wing headquarters.

"We'll get right on it!" Speedy responded.

Bea instructed Penny to quickly take the treasure chest to Commodore Smurkturkski and then rescue the crocodile.

Penny gave the treasure to the commodore. "Gotta go!" she said, and sped away to search for the crocodile in trouble.

"Thank you, Penny!" said Commodore Smurkturkski. "Now let's see the most beautiful treasure in the world!"

But before he could open the chest, Matilda snatched it and swam back toward the pirate ship!

Cap'n Dilly tossed a floating ring to Matilda, and she secured the treasure chest to it.

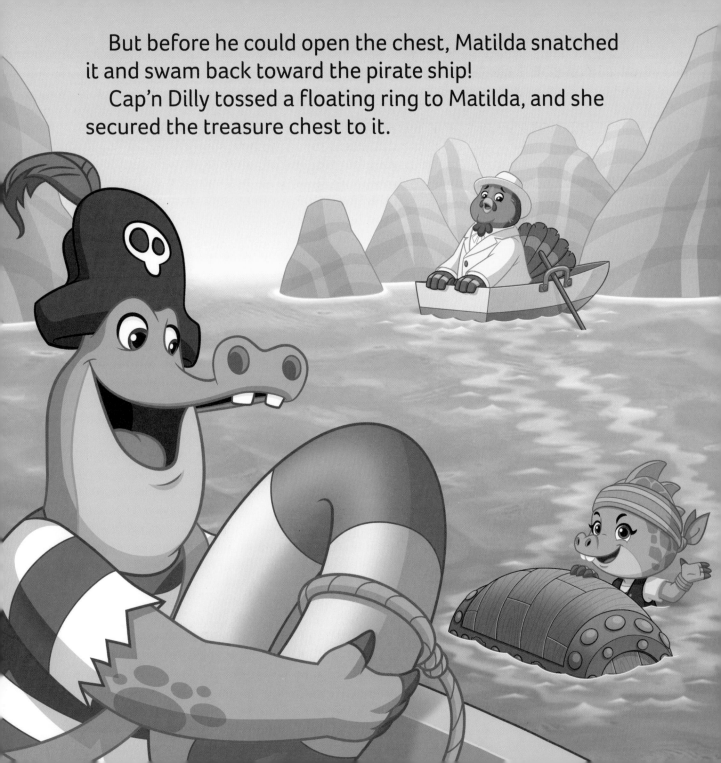

Then Matilda got on the ship, and the two pirate crocodiles sailed off.

"Wait! Come back with my treasure!" shouted Commodore Smurkturkski.

He leapt onto the chest. "Wait! Come back! Help!" he cried.

Penny heard the commodore and chased after the pirate ship.

"Oh! Those croc pirates tricked us!" Bea shouted.

"And they have the treasure!" said Speedy. He asked Swift and Brody to help out.

"Time to earn our wings, Brody!" Swift exclaimed.

The cadets raced to their vehicles and geared up.

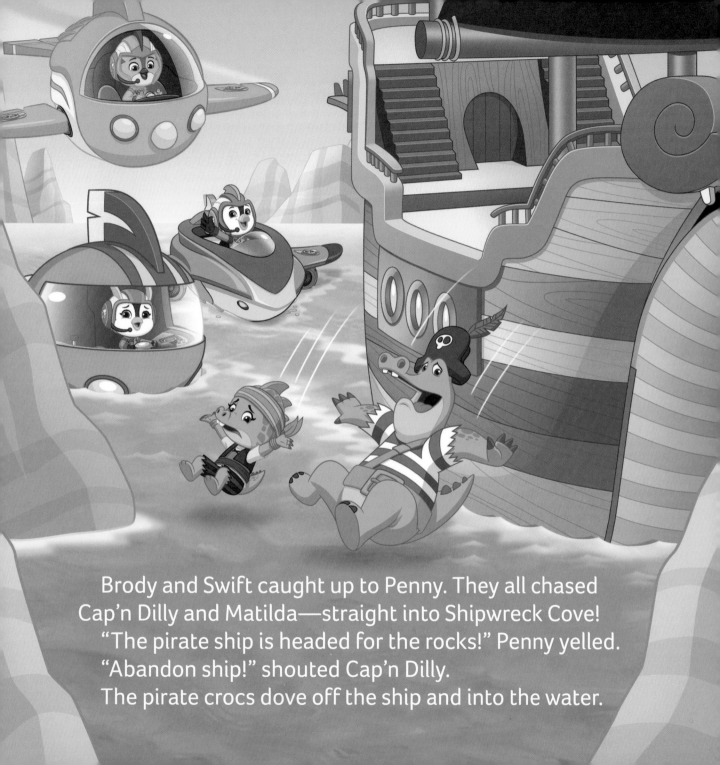

Brody and Swift caught up to Penny. They all chased
Cap'n Dilly and Matilda—straight into Shipwreck Cove!
"The pirate ship is headed for the rocks!" Penny yelled.
"Abandon ship!" shouted Cap'n Dilly.
The pirate crocs dove off the ship and into the water.

The cadets flew into action!

Swift landed his Flash Wing on the pirate ship's mast. He used his turbo jets to quickly turn the ship and stop it from crashing into the rocks. Penny used her Aqua Wing's claw to cut the towrope and grab the treasure chest. Brody rescued Commodore Smurkturkski with his Splash Wing.

"Oh, that wasn't part of my plan," Cap'n Dilly said, disappointed.

"You mean *arrr* plan," Matilda replied sadly.

Back at the Lemon Shack, the cadets and their friends gathered around the treasure chest.

"Penny was in charge of saving the treasure . . . but she ended up *gobba-gobba* saving *me*!" cheered Commodore Smurkturkski.

"I just did what any cadet would do," said Penny, smiling.

Commodore Smurkturkski opened the treasure chest to find . . . a little golden pirate ship! It was the best sunken treasure ever!